WINNIE-
THE-POOH
AND SOME BEES

WINNIE-THE-POOH AND SOME BEES

A.A. MILNE

illustrated by
ERNEST H. SHEPARD

METHUEN CHILDREN'S BOOKS

WINNIE-THE-POOH AND SOME BEES

Here is Edward Bear, coming downstairs now,
bump, bump, bump, on the back of his head,
behind Christopher Robin. It is, as far as he
knows, the only way of coming downstairs,

'*Winnie-the-Pooh wasn't quite sure,*' said *Christopher Robin.*

'*Now I am,*' said *a growly voice.*

'*Then I will go on,*' said *I.*)

One day when he was out walking, he came to an open place in the middle of the forest, and in the middle of this place was a large oak-tree, and, from the top of the tree, there came a loud buzzing-noise.

Winnie-the-Pooh sat down at the foot of
the tree, put his head between his paws,
and began to think.

First of all he said to himself: 'That buzzing-noise means something. You don't get
a buzzing-noise like that, just buzzing
and buzzing, without its meaning something.
If there's a buzzing-noise, somebody's
making a buzzing-noise, and the only reason
for making a buzzing-noise that *I* know of is
because you're a bee.'

Then he thought another long time, and
said: 'And the only reason for being a bee
that I know of is making honey.'

And then he got up, and said: 'And the
only reason for making honey is so as *I*
can eat it.'

So he began to climb the tree.

He
climbed
and he
climbed
and he
climbed,
and
as he
climbed
he sang
a little
song
to
himself.
It
went
like
this:

Isn't it funny
How a bear likes honey?
Buzz! Buzz! Buzz!
I wonder why he does?

Then he climbed a little further . . . and a little further . . . and then just a little further. By that time he had thought of another song.

It's a very funny thought that, if Bears were Bees,
They'd build their nests at the *bottom* of trees.
And that being so (if the Bees were Bears),
We shouldn't have to climb up all these stairs.

He was getting rather tired by this time, so that is why he sang a Complaining Song. He was nearly there now, and if he just stood on that branch . . . *Crack!*

'Oh, help!' said Pooh, as he dropped ten feet to the branch below him.

'If only I hadn't—' he said, as he bounced twenty feet on to the next branch.

'You see, what I *meant* to do,' he explained, as he turned head-over-heels, and crashed on to another branch thirty feet below, 'what I *meant* to do—'

'Of course, it *was* rather—' he admitted, as he slithered very quickly through the next six branches.

'It all comes, I suppose,' he decided, as he said good-bye to the last branch, spun round three times, and flew gracefully into a gorse-bush,

'it all comes of *liking* honey so much. Oh, help!'

He crawled out of the gorse-bush, brushed

the prickles from his nose, and began to think
again. And the first person he thought of was
Christopher Robin.

*('Was that me?' said Christopher Robin in an
awed voice, hardly daring to believe it.*

'That was you.'

*Christopher Robin said nothing, but his eyes
got larger and larger, and his face got pinker and
pinker.)*

So Winnie-the-Pooh went round to his friend
Christopher Robin, who lived behind a green
door in another part of the Forest.

'Good morning, Christopher Robin,' he said.

'Good morning, Winnie-*ther*-Pooh,' said you.

'I wonder if you've got such a thing as a balloon about you?'

'A balloon?'

'Yes, I just said to myself coming along: "I wonder if Christopher Robin has such a thing as a balloon about him?" I just said it to myself, thinking of balloons, and wondering.'

'What do you want a balloon for?' you said.

Winnie-the-Pooh looked round to see that nobody was listening, put his paw to his mouth, and said in a deep whisper: *'Honey!'*

'But you don't get honey with balloons!'

'I do,' said Pooh.

Well, it just happened that you had been to a party the day before at the house of your friend Piglet, and you had balloons at the party. You had had a big green balloon; and one of Rabbit's relations had had a big blue one,

and had left it behind, being really too young to go to a party at all; and so you had brought the green one *and* the blue one home with you.

'Which one would you like?' you asked Pooh.

He put his head between his paws and thought very carefully.

'It's like this,' he said. 'When you go after honey with a balloon, the great thing is not to let the bees know you're coming. Now, if you have a green balloon, they might think you were only part of the tree, and not notice you, and if you have a blue balloon, they might think you were only part of the sky, and not notice you, and the question is: Which is most likely?'

'Wouldn't they notice *you* underneath the balloon?' you asked.

'They might or they might not,' said Winnie-the-Pooh. 'You never can tell with bees.' He thought for a moment and said: 'I shall try to look like a small black cloud. That will deceive them.'

'Then you had better have the blue balloon,' you said; and so it was decided.

Well, you both went out with the blue balloon, and you took your gun with you, just in case, as you always did, and Winnie-the-Pooh went to a very muddy place that he knew of, and

rolled and rolled until he was black all over; and

then, when the balloon was blown up as big as big, and you and Pooh were both holding on to the string, you let go suddenly, and Pooh

Bear floated gracefully up into the sky, and stayed there – level with the top of the tree and about twenty feet away from it.

'Hooray!' you shouted.

'Isn't that fine?' shouted Winnie-the-Pooh down to you. 'What do I look like?'

'You look like a Bear holding on to a balloon,' you said.

'Not,' said Pooh anxiously, '—not like a small black cloud in a blue sky?'

'Not very much.'

'Ah, well, perhaps from up here it looks different. And, as I say, you never can tell with bees.'

There was no wind to blow him nearer to the tree so there he stayed. He could see the honey, he could smell the honey, but he couldn't quite reach the honey.

After a little while he called down to you.

'Christopher Robin!' he said in a loud whisper.

'Hallo!'

'I think the bees *suspect* something!'

'What sort of thing?'

'I don't know. But something tells me that they're *suspicious*!'

'Perhaps they think that you're after their honey?'

'It may be that. You never can tell with bees.'

There was another little silence, and then he called down to you again.

'Christopher Robin!'

'Yes?'

'Have you an umbrella in your house?'

'I think so.'

'I wish you would bring it out here, and walk up and down with it, and look up at me every now and then, and say "Tut-tut, it looks like rain." I think, if you did that, it would help the deception which we are practising on these bees.'

Well, you laughed to yourself, 'Silly old Bear!' but you didn't say it aloud because you were so fond of him, and you went home for your umbrella.

'Oh, there you are!' called down Winnie-

the-Pooh, as soon as you got back to the tree.
'I was beginning to get anxious. I have
discovered that the bees are now definitely
Suspicious.'

'Shall I put my umbrella up?' you said.

'Yes, but wait a moment. We must be
practical. The important bee to deceive is the
Queen Bee. Can you see which is the Queen
Bee from down there?'

'No.'

'A pity. Well, now, if you walk up and down
with your umbrella, saying, "Tut-tut, it looks like
rain," I shall do what I can by singing a little
Cloud Song, such as a cloud might sing. . . . Go!'

So, while you walked up and down and
wondered if it would rain, Winnie-the-Pooh
sang this song:

> How sweet to be a Cloud
>   Floating in the Blue!
> Every little cloud
> *Always* sings aloud.

> 'How sweet to be a Cloud
>   Floating in the Blue!'
> It makes him very proud
> To be a little cloud.

The bees were still buzzing as suspiciously as ever. Some of them, indeed, left their nests and flew all round the cloud as it began the second verse of this song, and one bee sat down on the nose of the cloud for a moment, and then got up again.

'Christopher – *ow!* – Robin,' called out the cloud.

'Yes?'

'I have just been thinking, and I have come to a very important decision. *These are the wrong sort of bees.*'

'Are they?'

'Quite the wrong sort. So I should think they would make the wrong sort of honey, shouldn't you?'

'Would they?'

'Yes. So I think I shall come down.'

'How?' asked you.

Winnie-the-Pooh hadn't thought about this. If he let go of the string, he would fall – *bump* – and he didn't like the idea of that. So he thought

for a long time, and then he said:

'Christopher Robin, you must shoot the balloon with your gun. Have you got your gun?'

'Of course I have,' you said. 'But if I do that, it will spoil the balloon,' you said.

'But if you *don't*,' said Pooh, 'I shall have to let go, and that would spoil *me*.'

When he put it like this, you saw how it was, and you aimed very carefully at the balloon, and fired.

'*Ow!*' said Pooh.

'Did I miss?' you asked.

'You didn't exactly *miss*,' said Pooh, 'but you missed the *balloon*.'

'I'm so sorry,' you said, and you fired again, and this time you hit the balloon, and the air came slowly out, and Winnie-the-Pooh floated down to the ground.

But his arms were so stiff from holding on to the

string of the balloon all that time that they stayed up straight in the air for more than a week, and whenever a fly came and settled on his nose he had to blow it off. And I think – but I am not sure – that *that* is why he was always called Pooh.

'Is that the end of the story?' asked Christopher Robin.

'That's the end of that one. There are others.'

'About Pooh and Me?'

'And Piglet and Rabbit and all of you. Don't you remember?'

'I do remember, and then when I try to remember, I forget.'

'That day when Pooh and Piglet tried to catch the Heffalump—'

'They didn't catch it, did they?'

'No.'

'Pooh couldn't, because he hasn't any brain. Did *I* catch it?'

'Well, that comes into the story.'

Christopher Robin nodded.

'I do remember,' he said, 'only Pooh doesn't very well, so that's why he likes having it told to him again. Because then it's a real story and not just a remembering.'

'That's just how *I* feel,' I said.

Christopher Robin gave a deep sigh, picked his Bear up by the leg, and walked off to the door, trailing Pooh behind him. At the door he turned and said, 'Coming to see me have my bath?'

'I might,' I said.

'I didn't hurt him when I shot him, did I?'

'Not a bit.'

He nodded and went out, and in a moment I heard Winnie-the-Pooh – *bump, bump, bump* – going up the stairs behind him.

Winnie-the-Pooh and Some Bees
is taken from *Winnie-the-Pooh*
originally published in
Great Britain 14 October 1926
by Methuen & Co. Ltd
Text by A.A. Milne and line drawings by Ernest H. Shepard
copyright under the Berne Convention

First published in this edition 1990
by Methuen Children's Books
an imprint of Reed Children's Books
Michelin House, 81 Fulham Road, London SW3 6RB
and Auckland, Melbourne, Singapore and Toronto
Reprinted 1991 (twice), 1992 (twice), 1994, 1995

Printed in Hong Kong

ISBN 0 416 16582 6